Mr. and Mrs. Thief

Story and pictures by

Naomi Kojima

Thomas Y. Crowell • New York

Designed by Ellen Weiss

LC-79-7902
ISBN 0-690-04021-0
ISBN 0-690-04022-9 (L.B.)

10 9 8 7 6 5 4 3 2 1
First Edition

For Richard Wood
& Mr. and Mrs. Thief,
who lived on Maury Street
(also for Seiichiro,
who lived next door to them)

Mr. and Mrs. Thief lived next door to me. They were *real thieves*, like the ones you read about in newspapers and see on TV. Mom would get mad at me when I said that, but it's true, because Old Chief told me so. Old Chief knows everything around this neighborhood.

Every evening they'd come out on the porch
and sit there for a long time, doing nothing.
I pretended like I was playing with my dog,
but I was watching them real carefully,
because even though they weren't doing
anything, I knew they were making plans.

I watched Mrs. Thief hang up her laundry...

...I watched Mr. Thief work on his car, every day. He had to keep it tuned up for quick getaways. I always knew he was saving it for a really big job, though, because I never saw him take it anywhere.

Every night I wrote down all the important things I discovered about them in my notebook.

Once while I was patrolling around their house on my bicycle, Mrs. Thief called me over and gave me two cookies, one for me and one for my dog. Oh, oh, I thought—what if they know I'm on their trail? She smiled real big and I had to eat it—but I crossed my fingers behind my back, and that's why we both didn't die.

Sometimes they would leave the house for the whole day...

...and when they came back, they'd have boxes and bags full of strange things.

I was pretty sure they hid their loot in the wall, because Mr. Thief was always patching up cracks.

One day I saw them at a store. They were
buying some rope, a crowbar, a glass cutter,
a rasp, a flashlight, a ladder, and two pairs
of gloves.

I thought the storekeeper was going to get suspicious. But I guess Mr. and Mrs. Thief practiced staying cool in these situations, because the man didn't seem to notice anything, and they left the store without being caught.

Then one day Mr. Thief moved his big old station wagon out front. I thought they were finally going to pull that big job they'd been planning, maybe rob a bank. But instead, Mr. and Mrs. Thief carried out all their furniture, and their boxes and bags full of things, and moved away.

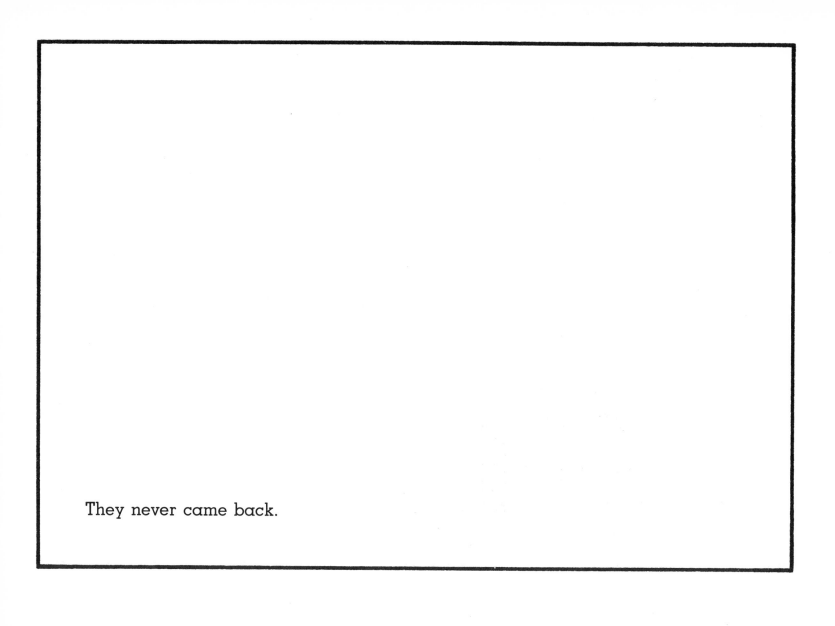

They never came back.

I'm sure there must still be some of their loot holed up in there. I keep thinking I ought to sneak in and poke around, but I haven't done that yet, and now there are new neighbors coming in and I'll probably never have the chance.

The new neighbors started moving some of
their stuff in yesterday. You should see them.
Old Chief has already checked them out,
and he says that from the look of things they
are definitely SPIES.

I'm just going to have to keep my guard up.